HARRY
the WOODPECKER'S Search for a Home

Story by Joy & Craig Johnson
Text by Joy Johnson
Watercolor illustrations & layout by Craig Johnson

FSC
www.fsc.org

MIX
Paper from
responsible sources
FSC® C015782

Proudly printed in Seattle, Washington, USA

ORANGE SPOT PUBLISHING

Tap-a-tap-a-tap… tap-tap-tap… Harry the (Hairy) Woodpecker used his strong, wedge-shaped bill to chisel some finishing touches around the opening of a new nest cavity. His mate, Harriet, watched. After looking at many trees in the forest where they lived, they had chosen this one as the best in which to create this year's nest for their young. The pair took turns chipping away for two weeks, carrying off wood shavings with their bills. Now the nest cavity was nearly complete!

3

Early the next morning, a strange, deep rumble vibrated the trees. Then they heard a loud, high-pitched grinding noise. Alarmed, Harry and Harriet realized this might not be the best place to raise their family after all. They took to the air to see what was happening.

As Harry and Harriet flew overhead, a hard-working construction crew with a bright orange front-loader tractor and yellow excavator cleared and scraped the land below, getting ready to build new homes for *people* to live in.

Since it was nearly time for Harriet to lay her eggs, the woodpeckers hastily winged their way toward a forested area in the distance to find another tree for their nest.

Pileated
Woodpecker

Downy
Woodpecker

8

Upon reaching the forest, Harry and Harriet found that many other kinds of woodpeckers were already using this woodlot, so there was no space to build their nest.

Northern Flicker

Red-breasted Sapsucker

On they flew....

Gazing down through the clouds, they saw a large
neighborhood spread out before them. With great
relief, Harriet noticed one house had bird feeders
and water available so they could rest and eat
before pressing on.

Flying ahead, Harry spotted an enormous old snag. By tapping and probing with his bill, he found this dead tree could easily be chiseled to create a cavity. And there was another snag nearby. One of these would surely be right for their nest and the other would provide a place for Harriet to roost at night to keep safe and warm.

Native trees and shrubs along the yard's edge would supply insects and berries to eat. There was even a birdbath with fresh water behind the house.

At last, Harry had found the perfect location for their new home!

13

Cut-away view
of nest cavity

14

Since the snag was dead, it was softer on the inside than a live tree and they could dig out a cavity rather quickly. Soon the nest was finished and Harriet laid four eggs.

During the day, the pair took turns incubating the eggs, sitting on them to keep them warm until they hatched. Harry always stayed in the nest at night while Harriet roosted in the other tree cavity they had made nearby.

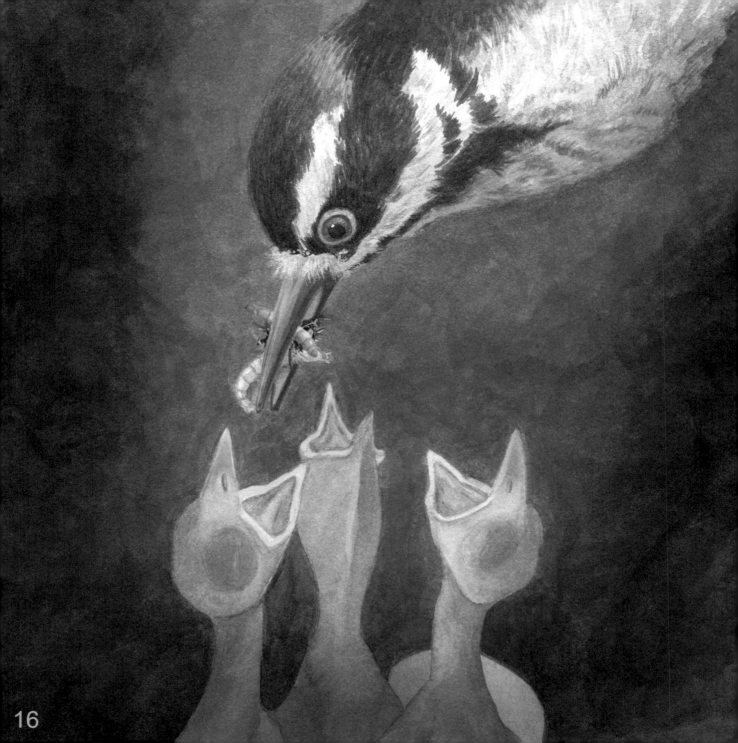

After 18 days, the eggs began to crack open. Out came three hungry hatchlings! (The fourth egg never hatched, which sometimes happens.)

Throughout the day, either Harry or Harriet stayed in the nest brooding, keeping the chicks warm until their feathers grew. Meanwhile, the other partner searched for food, returning several times each hour to feed the hungry babies' gaping mouths.

It would be a week before the three baby birds could see. But whenever mom or dad entered the nest hole, the nestlings instantly stretched their pink necks as far as possible, all raspy young voices begging to be fed. This time, Harry reached in to meet them with soft, squishy larvae in his bill.

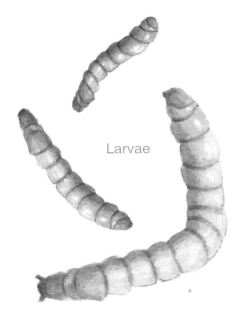

Larvae

One warm day, after spending almost a month in the dim coziness of the nest, Harry Jr. was especially eager for an insect meal. Awkwardly, he inched his way up the wall of the tree cavity, using his flexible feet and sharp claws. Finally reaching the opening, he was the first of the three young birds to poke his head through the hole and peer out at the world beyond. Quickly, Harry Jr. was rewarded with a delivery of ants and beetles from his father!

Just a few days later, Harry Jr. and his sisters, Hanna and Hope, all made their way out of the cavity and onto the outside of the nest tree.

Beetles & ant

Not quite ready to find their own food, the siblings clumsily flew to nearby trees where they would cling to the trunk or a branch, waiting for their parents to come back with a meal.

Harriet

Hope

Harry Jr.

20

Once all the youngsters could fly, Harry and Harriet took the family around to explore places to forage and find water. Usually two kids would go with one parent and one kid with the other.

Hanna

Harry

21

While searching for food, the devoted parents stayed alert to dangers, giving the young birds sharp, loud *peek, peek* warning calls when threats were close by.

Cooper's Hawk

After spending several weeks with their parents, learning how to care for themselves, the three young woodpeckers were ready to venture out on their own.

Using his newly acquired skills, Harry Jr. gently tapped on the outside of a tree, listening for the hollow sound of insect tunnels beneath the bark. Locating one, he chiseled into the tree bark with his bill, using a side-to-side motion.

Once he had made a small hole, he reached in with his long tongue. Feeling around with the sensitive tip, he found a marshmallow-like larva and pierced it with the pointed end of his tongue. Sticky saliva and barbs that spread out on his tongue tip helped him pull out the tasty meal.

Woodpecker
tongue

Eventually leaving his parents' territory to live on his own, Harry Jr. found a place not far away with some large trees for shelter and insects. Plus a kind family had put out bird feeders with suet and peanuts. These were particularly helpful for him during cold winter months when it was harder to find food.

In springtime, Harry Jr. and his sisters would all try to find mates and raise their own families… but those will be new stories. Meanwhile, the adventures of life continue.

Woodpecker Facts

1. Smallest of all North American woodpeckers, Downy Woodpeckers' old nest cavities are used by small song birds, like chickadees and nuthatches.

2. Hairy Woodpeckers are named for the soft, whitish feathers on their backs, which probably looked like hair to the person who named them.

3. Red-breasted Sapsuckers are known as a *keystone species*. This is because of the sap-wells and nest cavities they create which are also used by other birds and animals.

4. Ants make up about 80% of the Northern Flicker's diet. They find ants on the ground, on stumps and at the base of trees.

5. Pileated means crested or capped. A Pileated Woodpecker may strike a wood surface with its bill about 12,000 times in one day!

For more facts, please visit: www.pugetsoundbackyardbirds.com